RUSH HOUR

AN EROTIC ADVENTURE

VICTORIA RUSH

VOLUME 5

JADE'S EROTIC ADVENTURES - BOOK 5

COPYRIGHT

OTHER BOOKS BY VICTORIA RUSH:

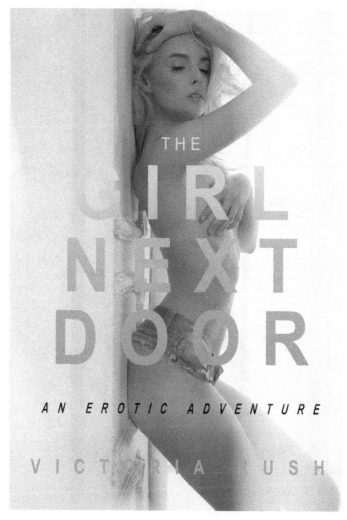

THE
GIRL
NEXT
DOOR

AN EROTIC ADVENTURE

VICTORIA RUSH

Spying on the neighbors just got a lot more interesting...

GIRLS' CAMP

AN EROTIC ADVENTURE

VICTORIA RUSH

Getting wet was never this much fun...

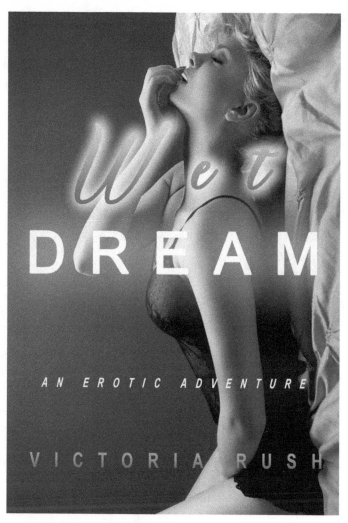

Wet

DREAM

AN EROTIC ADVENTURE

VICTORIA RUSH

There's only one place you can live out your wildest fantasies...

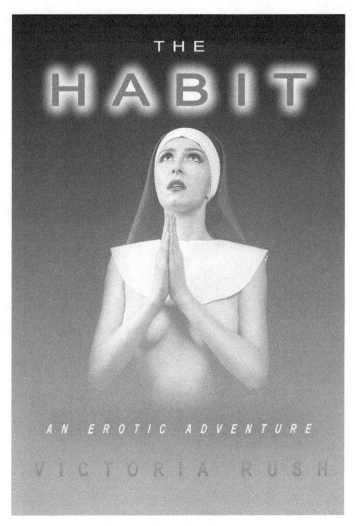

THE
HABIT

AN EROTIC ADVENTURE

VICTORIA RUSH

Some habits are harder to break than others...

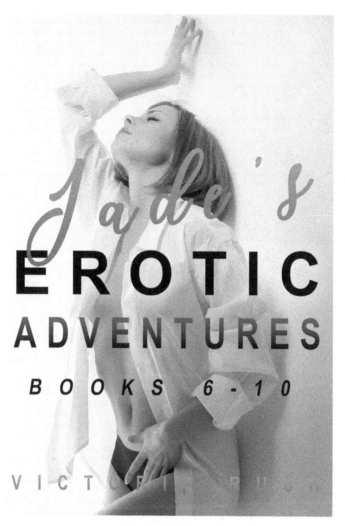

Jade's
EROTIC
ADVENTURES

BOOKS 6 - 10

VICTORIA RUSH

Books 6 - 10 in the bestselling series - now 60% off.

For the uninhibited...

1

DANGEROUS LIAISONS

I'd been looking forward to my first visit to New York City for months. After hearing so much about The Big Apple from TV shows, movies, and friends, I'd crammed a busy itinerary into my short one-week stay. Broadway, the Metropolitan Museum, Rockefeller Center, shopping on 5th Avenue—there was so much to do in so little time.

But first, there was the little matter of my three-day business conference. The largest graphic design trade show of the year was running at the Javits Center in midtown Manhattan, and it was something I felt I couldn't pass up. Besides displaying all the latest technology in the ever-changing landscape of graphic design software, all the big media companies would be there. As a freelance artist, there were simply too many potential customers to ignore.

It would have been easier to take a cab to get to my venue, but today I wanted to experience an authentic New York rite of passage by taking the subway. As I walked down the front steps of my hotel toward the 103rd Street subway station one block away, I marveled at the majestic trees lining Central Park West. The city park was definitely on my to-do list, and I planned to take a long stroll later in the day to absorb the autumn color.

When I descended the stairs to the underground concourse, I was surprised how busy the station was. There was a heavy flow of commuters streaming into the station, and the subway platform was already four or five people deep waiting for the next rush hour train to arrive. I purchased a MetroCard at one of the vending machines, then scurried through the turnstiles onto the packed platform.

Suddenly, the station filled with a deafening roar as two trains raced into the terminal from opposite ends. The southbound train screeched to a halt in front of me and opened its doors, and a small group of people shuffled off the train. Then the dense crowd on the platform converged on the narrow opening, trying to squeeze into the tight cabin. I wasn't prepared for the aggressiveness of the passengers as they pushed and jostled past me toward the door. Within ten seconds, the car was filled to capacity as a wall of passengers stood by the lip of the door, blocking the opening.

Holy crap, I thought. *My friends weren't kidding when they said everything moves faster in Manhattan.*

I stepped back from the opening and watched the passengers squeeze their shoulders together to allow enough room for the door to close.

At least next time, I breathed a sigh of relief, *I'll be at the front of the line.*

Within a minute, another train roared into the station. I quickly stepped to the side of the door nearest me and waited for the exiting passengers to leave the compartment. When I stepped into the carriage, I noticed it was already half full. The surge of passengers streaming in behind me pushed me deeper into the car and off to the side. The seats were already taken, so I found a spot in the corner beside the exit door and grabbed hold of the overhead support bar to steady myself. A pretty brunette was seated in the single chair on the end wall, reading Cosmo.

"Excuse me," I said, wiggling in next to her, trying to find a spot with a few inches of personal space.

She smiled at me and nodded, then returned her attention to her magazine. Passengers continued filtering into the subway car, pushing and squeezing us closer together. By the time the doors closed, I scarcely had an inch to breathe, and I could feel bodies pressing up against me from the sides and behind. I grasped the overhead bar more firmly and spread my feet a few inches to get a solid footing. I glanced at the people resting on the seats below me and noticed that everyone was either tapping on their cell phones or reading a newspaper.

When the train picked up speed and was swallowed in the blackness of the underground tunnel, I looked in the reflected light of the window in front of me to scan the activity in my car. Everybody seemed to be staring impassively ahead or reading the advertisements above the windows. As the train rattled through the tunnel jostling back and forth, I could feel the surrounding passengers shifting their weight against me. Someone's hips were pressing into my ass, and I looked in the window to see a pretty college-aged girl wearing a backpack with the NYU logo. The feeling of having someone touching me so intimately in the tight confines of the subway car was turning me on, and I felt my pussy beginning to tingle.

I tilted my hips toward her to try to get her attention, but she seemed lost in conversation as her fingers flicked over her cellphone screen. Glancing to my side, I noticed the seated brunette had lifted her gaze from her magazine and was watching my ass rubbing against the college girl's hips directly in front of her. She looked up in my direction, then turned to our reflected image in the window and smiled at me. I blushed at the realization that she'd caught me trying to grab a cheap feel on the subway train and quickly turned my head in the other direction. But there was something about the way she looked at me that got my juices flowing even stronger.

When the train entered the next station and our car doors opened, I was sad to see the college girl leave the compartment. A new surge of passengers boarded the cabin, then the brunette stuffed her magazine in her purse and stood up to take a position on my left side. She was so close to me, I could smell her perfume. She reached onto the support handle and grasped the bar beside my hand. The feeling of her warm skin next to mine on the cool bar sent a charge through my body.

Another passenger squeezed in behind us, taking her vacant seat on the end wall, and I glanced at the brunette in the window reflection and smiled. She was a little younger than me, maybe in her early thirties, and dressed in a tight-fitting business suit that hugged her curvy body. She had big brown eyes and sexy full lips, and I blushed when she caught me checking out her body.

We were packed like sardines in the tight confines of the subway car, and I felt the brunette's hips press against the side of my ass. I wasn't sure if she was doing it intentionally or just trying to provide some more space for the last few passengers squeezing into our end of the car. Either way, it was a pleasant feeling, and I kept my feet firmly planted and my body erect, maintaining the pressure between us.

When the train left the station and accelerated into the tunnel, the shifting weight of the carriage caused our bodies to bump together, creating a different kind of friction between us. I could feel her hard pubis pushing against my cheeks, and I squeezed my glutes to provide a firmer surface for her to get more direct stimulation. To my delight, she began moving her hips rhythmically against my ass, and I felt her wetness soaking through the thin microfiber on the back of my pants.

She was tribbing me in the tight confines of the subway car, with nobody the wiser!

I looked in the car window and gave her a knowing smile, then to remove all doubt as to whether I was a willing participant in the equation, I began moving my hips in rhythm with hers. If there was anything I could do to help her get off in the secrecy of our confined space, I was only too happy to help. The pace of her gyrations began to pick up and as her mouth parted, I could feel the coolness of her breath against my neck. She interlaced her fingers with mine on the overhead bar and squeezed my hand. As we watched each other in the reflected glass, her mouth opened wider and the look on her face contorted in sweet agony.

By now, my own pussy was flooded with lubrication, and I could feel the wetness accumulating in my panties. I was dying for some stimulation of my own, but I couldn't move my free hand in direct view of the seated passengers in front of me. Even though they seemed preoccupied with other matters, it was simply too risky. I tried to reach behind me with my right hand to touch the brunette, but she was on the wrong side. All I could do was squeeze my left butt cheek to provide a hard surface for her to rub against and provide a little extra stimulation by tilting my hips quietly in rhythm with her.

Suddenly, she stopped moving, as she pressed her pussy firmly against my backside and squeezed my hand tightly on the bar. I saw her head bob forward in a series of spastic lurches as she grimaced trying to stifle her pleasure.

I'd never seen anything so hot in my entire life. The notion of having sex on a crowded train, even between two fully-clothed people, was insanely arousing. This was my first experience with illicit public sex, and I was already addicted. Even my experiences on the Nude Cruise couldn't match this, knowing that everybody already had tacit approval to engage in public sex in the erotic-themed venues. But sex on a *train* was a definite no-no, where one or both of us could be charged with a crime, especially if it was found to be nonconsensual.

But this was definitely *consensual*. I was more than a willing partner, and I wanted *more*.

I was glad when the train roared into the next station, providing a bit of a distraction. It gave me a chance to shift position with the pretty brunette, so we could reciprocate favors. As people began to shuffle out of our car, I stepped aside to give her some space to move in front of me. This would have given me a bit more privacy and an opportunity to stimulate my own clit, but she reached out and pressed her hand gently against my back. Apparently, she had other ideas. I wasn't sure what she had in mind, and I frowned as a new round of passengers crowded into our end of the car, pressing us together in the previous position.

I looked in the window and furrowed my eyebrows at the brunette, wondering what she was thinking. She simply smiled at me and blew me a silent kiss as she pressed her hips against my pliant ass. This time, as soon as the train entered the darkened tunnel, I felt her right hand circle under my buttocks and two fingers press into the opening between my legs.

God, yes! I thought, catching my breath from her intrusion into my private zone.

I glanced at the two people seated directly in front of me to see if they'd noticed the unusual movement only two feet away from them at their same eye level. A young woman was busy texting on her phone and a businessman had his head buried in the spread of the New York Times, oblivious to what was going on around them. And the people standing beside me were either peering at the ads on the wall or reading their phones.

Thank God for smartphones.

The brunette now had a green light to pretty much do whatever she wanted with me in the tight confines of our noisy subway car. Nobody could see or hear what was going on below their line of sight. I spread my feet a few inches further apart to give her freer access to my underside, then tilted my hips back to move my throbbing clit closer to her hand. My pants were now thoroughly soaked through with my love juices, and the brunette slid her fingers through the cleft in my labia created by the tight seam of my dress pants.

How I wished I'd worn a skirt instead of pants on this first day of the conference!

But it didn't really matter since she probably could have gotten me off even if I was wearing a chastity belt, I was so worked up by now. I looked at her in the glass, and she winked at me as she rolled my erect clit between her thumb and her forefinger. I gasped out loud, then coughed a few times when some of the seated passengers looked up, trying to divert attention from what was going on. The brunette paused briefly until everybody's attention returned to their reading material.

Not knowing how much longer we'd have before being interrupted at the next stop or if someone might catch on to what we were doing, I was eager to get off as soon as possible. I parted my legs another inch and tilted my hips back as far as I could to signal that I was ready. The brunette looked at me intently in the window then she began to rub my clit more firmly. I closed my eyes and exhaled from the pleasure emanating between my legs and began to sway my hips in tandem with the movement of her fingers.

I began to hear the familiar echo sound of the train approached another station, and I squeezed my buttock muscles to speed the arrival of my orgasm. Just as the train raced into the new station, I felt the passion engulf me, and I clamped down on the brunette's fingers and bit my tongue, trying to stifle my moans. I'd never had to work so hard to conceal the powerful orgasm washing over me. The contractions seemed to go on forever, and I was worried I'd still be coming as people began to shuffle off the train.

But the timing was perfect, and the last waves of my orgasm subsided just as the train came to a stop. But by this time, I was so worried that someone might have noticed us, that I pulled away from the overhead bar and began making my way off the train. I hated to leave the brunette so abruptly, but I was too embarrassed that we'd be found out. Besides, I couldn't continue on to my business conference with this giant wet spot between my legs. I'd have to go back to my hotel for a change of clothes before going any further.

As I got off the car and headed toward the station exit to catch a cab, I paused in the middle of the platform and turned around as the train began to pull away. The brunette and I made eye contact, and we smiled at one another. We'd shared a powerful silent connection that would forever stay between the two of us.

2

DRESS UP

That night I could hardly sleep. I couldn't stop thinking about what had happened on the subway. I came three more times visualizing the memory of the brunette fingering me on the crowded train. It wasn't just the idea of having public sex that turned me on, it was the *danger* of the act that brought it to a new level. If either one of us had been caught, we could have been charged with indecent behavior and led out of the station in handcuffs. When I finally did nod off, I dreamt of being fondled by multiple strangers, surrounded by oblivious travelers focused on other distractions.

I woke up with a giant wet spot on the sheets and staggered to the shower to get ready in time for day two of my conference. I figured the previous day's encounter was a once-in-a-lifetime fluke, where I just happened to find myself next to someone bold enough to make a brazen public advance. But I planned to be ready just in case. I wore a loose-fitting summer dress with no bra or panties, and three-inch platform sandals to provide easier access to my undercarriage. This time, there'd be no need to rush back to my hotel to change my soiled undergarments. Even if I wasn't able to hook up with the pretty brunette again, just the sensation of feeling the swirling air from the moving train on my bare pussy would be a thrill.

I knew it was a longshot that I'd find the brunette in the same place on the same train on two consecutive days. But she looked like a regular commuter, and I figured that if I timed it right, I might get lucky. I glanced at my watch and noticed that it was 7:30. I grabbed my purse and rushed out of my hotel room, already feeling the moisture building between my legs.

When I got to the subway station, I slipped my Metro-Card through the card reader then paused to get my bearings. I remembered turning to the right yesterday after passing through the turnstiles to get away from the crowd, but I couldn't recall how far down the platform I'd gone before getting on the train. Then I noticed a familiar advertisement on the side wall. I walked toward it and stepped forward to get closer to the edge of the platform. I didn't want to risk missing my train twice in as many days.

After a few minutes, a train rattled into the station, and I swiveled my head trying to catch sight of the pretty brunette in one of the passing cars. But it was moving too fast and the cars were too full to make out any familiar faces. When the train came to a halt, I scanned inside the adjacent car, but I didn't see the brunette. I hesitated, unsure whether to enter the compartment.

Had I missed her train? I thought. *Was I too early, or too late? Should I wait for the next one to see if I can find her on that one?*

I searched frantically through the window at the south end of the carriage, but it was too densely packed with passengers to make anything out. Thinking she'd taken another seat out of view, I stepped into the car just before the door closed. As the train sped out of the station, I pushed my way through the crowd toward the end wall. When I got to the far corner, I was disappointed to see no sign of the brunette. I squeezed toward the window and grabbed hold of the overhead support bar. To my surprise, the same college girl who'd been standing behind me yesterday was seated on the bench in front of me, reading a book.

I craned my head toward the other end of the cabin to look for any sign of the brunette. Just when I was beginning to despair about ever seeing her again, a familiar scent tickled my nose. *That perfume! Could it be—.* I glanced in the window reflection and saw the brunette pushing her way through the crowd in my direction.

She was a creature of habit, after all. Or maybe she just had the same idea I had—that if she got on the same train at the same time in the same place, she might be lucky enough to find that special someone who shared her predilection for public sex.

When she came up beside me, she took the position as yesterday, just to my left and behind me. Then she reached up and placed her hand over mine on the overhead bar and smiled at me in the window. She ran her eyes up and down my body, noticing my change of clothes and nodded with approval. Then she pressed in closer behind me and I felt her hand reach under my dress and squeeze my butt cheek. My ass trembled in excitement at her touch, and I spread my legs as far as I could to give her more space to reach between my legs.

She wasted no time plunging three fingers into my aching snatch, and I gasped out loud in pleasure. The college girl glanced up from her book and I coughed into my hand to distract her attention. The brunette paused until everybody's attention returned to their reading material, then she resumed finger-fucking me. I leaned over to tilt my pussy in her direction and noticed the college girl was no longer peering down at her book. Her eyelashes fluttered under her brow as she stared straight ahead at my dress. I wasn't sure if she'd noticed the brunette's hand movement under my garment, or if she merely suspected what was going on. Either way, I began to get worried and stopped moving my hips while I stared into the brunette's eyes in the window, trying to signal for her to stop before we got caught.

Fortunately, the train roared into the next station providing a temporary diversion. As it began to spit out passengers and take on a fresh load, the brunette pulled her fingers out of my pussy and began circling my clit. She was enjoying watching me squirm, and she had no intention of stopping her little tease. I closed my eyes and bit my lip as the new crop of passengers squeezed and pushed in behind us.

I noticed the college girl hadn't gotten off at the same stop as yesterday and saw that she was still peering straight ahead at my dress. I looked up at the brunette, pleading for her to stop until the train left the station. At least in the relative privacy of the darkened tunnel, the increased noise and jostling of the train would provide a temporary distraction from prying eyes. I wasn't sure if the brunette had also noticed the college girl's diverted attention. She simply smiled at me in the window as if to say: *So what if someone notices? Live in the moment, and revel in the extra attention.*

When the train finally sped out of the station, I glanced at the subway map over the window and saw that our next stop was 86th Street. We wouldn't have long to finish our business before the next interruption. Sensing my concern, the brunette thrust her thumb into my pussy and began massaging my clit with the cup of her hand. I groaned softly and twisted my face in pleasure as she watched my tortured agony in the window.

I had to fight the temptation not to rock my hips, and I pushed down on her hand so she could fuck me deeper with her thumb. I was gushing all over her, and I was worried that someone might hear the suspicious sloshing sound emanating from between my legs. But the train must have been running behind schedule, and the sound of it racing through the noisy tunnel overpowered every other sound in the compartment.

I glanced down at the college girl and saw that she'd placed her book on her lap, cradling it open with two hands under its spine. Her knees were slightly parted, and her right hand was moving slowly under the book. She was touching herself while she watched the brunette finger me under my dress!

The image of the girl rubbing herself while I was being fucked from behind sent a jolt through my body, and I felt my pleasure suddenly starting to rise. I caught sight of myself in the window and saw the look of ecstasy on my face and hoped that no one else was watching besides the brunette. My hard nipples were pressing against the loose cotton of my sundress, and if anybody had bothered to look up from their cell phones, it would have been obvious exactly what was going on below their line of sight.

I could feel my orgasm rising and I clenched my face to mask the intense sensations gripping my body. I couldn't believe I was about to come again surrounded by hundreds of oblivious passengers. Well, not *every* passenger. The college girl's lips parted and her eyelashes began to flutter as she neared the peak of her own pleasure.

Suddenly, her chest jerked in a series of small rhythmic spasms. Seeing her come as she watched the brunette fuck me from behind opened my own floodgates. A powerful orgasm engulfed my body and I clenched my ass cheeks together, clamping down over the brunette's hand between my legs. She watched my suffering in the window as my pussy squeezed her thumb in a series of violent contractions. My climax seemed to go forever and I twisted my face, trying to mask the incredible feeling of ecstasy washing over me.

The decibel level in the cabin suddenly rose again as the train entered the next station, finally giving me a chance to exhale and catch my breath. I wondered if the college girl noticed the puddle of fluid on the floor directly underneath me and between her legs. By the time the train stopped, my pussy finally finished pulsing, and the brunette began to retrieve her hand from between my thighs.

As passengers began exiting the train, I reached into my purse and handed her a handkerchief. She wiped her hand with the cloth, then placed it in her pants pocket and squeezed in front of me. I was disappointed she was wearing another pantsuit today, but I understood her intention clearly. There was no way I was going to leave her hanging for a second day in a row. I was dying to return the favor and give her a silent orgasm of her own.

But it wouldn't be quite as easy to disguise my attention, especially to the passengers seated directly in front of us on the bench. The college girl was flanked by two middle-aged businessmen reading the New York Times. If either one of them lowered their paper and looked up, they could easily detect the movement of my hand between the brunette's parted legs. The brunette must have been thinking the same thing, because she ducked under my outstretched arm and shifted over to my other side, directly in front of the college girl.

So she *had* noticed the girl's attention after all!

She reached up to grasp the overhead bar with her left hand and placed it next to mine. We'd switched positions now and I was the one who had clear access to her ass and erogenous regions with my dominant hand. When the train picked up speed and rocketed out of the station, I didn't waste any time. I didn't know what her regular stop was, but I looked up at the map and saw that the Javits Center stop was only four stops away. If I was going to get the brunette off in time not to miss the start of my conference for a second day, I had to get to work quickly.

When the train entered the tunnel, I moved my hand behind her ass and slipped my fingers into the crack between her legs. I gasped when I felt the moist opening of her bare slit. *Clever girl!* She'd opened the seam between her pant legs just enough for me to slip two fingers inside her. I glanced at her in the window and rejoiced as I thrust my middle and forefinger deep into her pussy. She closed her eyes and parted her legs as I felt her left pinky finger twitch on the bar next to mine.

From my new position two feet further to the side, I could now see the side of the college girl's face clearly. She was staring straight ahead, watching the movement of my hand between the brunette's parted legs. From her position directly in front of the brunette, she had a clear view of my fingers buried inside her pussy. She glanced out the corner of her eyes to ensure her seatmates were still distracted by their papers, then spread her legs gently apart. Her right hand then disappeared under her book, and when I glanced at the brunette in the window, I saw that her attention was also riveted on the girl.

I could feel the brunette's pussy growing wetter, and a soft moan emanated from her closed mouth. I smiled at the thought of her and the college girl sharing a moment, then I pulled my forefingers out of her pussy and inserted my pinky and ring fingers in their place. As I began to fuck her with my two little fingers, I pushed my forefingers forward until I found her hard nub pressing against her trousers. The college girl now had a commanding view of my fingers working the brunette's clit, while the rest of my hand fucked her hard from behind. I could feel the brunette's hips swaying as I pushed my fingers in and out of her, and the pace of her breathing increasing between her parted her lips.

Just when I thought I might be able to get her off before we hit the next stop, the train roared into the 72nd Street station. The businessmen on opposite sides of the college girl glanced up from their papers to check the station and I quickly retracted my fingers from the front of the brunette's pussy to ensure they wouldn't notice. As the passengers began to thin out beside us, I removed the rest of my hand, worried that someone might wonder what it was doing positioned so far under the brunette's ass.

It wasn't quite as easy to disguise our activity as it had been under my dress. I checked the subway map to see how long the distance was to our next stop at Columbus Circle. Then I looked at the brunette in the window and nodded, indicating that we'd have a little more time alone in the next tunnel. When I peered down at the college girl, I caught her glancing at me. I smiled at her, but she quickly lowered her head in embarrassment.

When the train left the 72nd Street Station, I glanced at the two businessmen to make sure the coast was clear, then I inserted my fingers back inside the brunette's slit. There was something about this combination of finger action that was getting me turned on, and I hoped the brunette was enjoying it as much as I was. As I thrust my little fingers into her pussy, my two forefingers pinched her clit under her trousers and I began to thrust them forward and backward.

The brunette's mouth parted and her eyes flitted with pleasure. Her cunt clamped over my fingers as she fucked my hand with her swaying hips. I glanced at the college girl and saw that her lips were parted as she panted softly, watching me finger the brunette just inches away from her face. I knew the brunette would want to make this last as long as possible, but as the train neared Columbus Circle, the pace of her hip movements sped up and the walls of her pussy pressed tighter around my fingers. As we swung into the station, her eyes flew open and she locked eyes on me as a flush rolled over her cheeks and she jerked her hips in a series of rhythmic spasms.

I glanced at the girl and saw her mouth wide open in a silent gag, almost like she was about to be sick. But I knew it was a different kind of sickness she was feeling, as she experienced her own private *petite mort*. Realizing I'd just made two beautiful women come together on a crowded subway train, my own pussy began pulsing in an involuntary orgasm. As our carriage rolled to a stop in the station, the brunette reached into her pocket and handed me my soiled kerchief. I held it to my nose briefly pretending to wipe my nose, then quietly cleaned my hands as I soaked up the sweet bouquet of our forbidden love.

3

DOWN AND DIRTY

W hen I got back to my hotel after the conference ended that day, I tore off my sundress and plunged my favorite vibrator deep inside my aching pussy. The events from the morning's train ride had been running through my head all day, and I was desperate for release. When I came, I screamed out loud, happy to be freed from the unnatural restraints of the crowded subway car. As much as I loved all the danger and secrecy of our illicit public liaison, it had been supremely difficult stifling the pleasure I felt surrounded by so many people.

That night, I had so many scenarios running through my head, it took me a long time to fall asleep. I knew there was a good chance I'd find the pretty brunette and the college girl on the next day's train, and my mind raced with all the ways the three of us could have fun. The lack of privacy in the subway car would still constrain our level of engagement, but with the college girl expressing renewed interest, we had a whole new world of possibilities. I dreamt of the three of us bare naked, screwing each other in full view of the gawking passengers.

Even though I'd only packed the one dress for this trip, I didn't hesitate to wear it again for the third day of my conference. I didn't care if anyone recognized that I was repeating my wardrobe choice. All I cared about was making it as easy as possible for the brunette, and hopefully also the college girl, to get as close and deep into me as possible. This time, I wasn't taking any chances missing the brunette's train. I left my hotel room early that day, planning to wait for them on the station platform. Something told me they wouldn't be playing so coy hiding from me in the train compartment today.

I got to the station ten minutes early and staked out a spot in the same location on the platform. I checked each passing train for any sign of the brunette, and just as I anticipated, she was standing near the window when the 7:45 rolled in. She waved at me to get my attention, and I squeezed into the compartment and pushed my way through the crowd toward the far end. When I got to the corner, the college girl was sitting in her same seat in the middle of the bench, with the brunette standing directly in front of her grasping the overhead bar with two hands.

I squeezed in next to the brunette and smiled at her in the glass, then looked down at the college girl. She was still playing hard-to-get, averting eye contact with us, but I noticed that today she was wearing a knee-length skirt instead of jeans. I was disappointed to see the brunette still hadn't gotten with the program, wearing yet another business pantsuit. I shook my head and pinched my eyebrows in the window reflection to express my dismay, but she simply nodded and smiled back at me. The look on her face was different today, like she knew something I didn't.

I glanced down at the bench again to scope out the gallery and noticed the girl was flanked today by two other girls about her same age. I didn't see any NYU logos on their paraphernalia, but they both had backpacks resting on their knees. I wasn't sure what to make of the arrangement, then I noticed they were all tapping on their phones and giggling.

This complicates the picture, I thought.

The newspapers the businessmen were reading yesterday had provided some extra cover for our dangerous liaison, but now the entire bench had a clear view directly ahead of them. I glanced up at the brunette and directed my eyes in the girls' direction to indicate my concern, but she shook her head and mouthed the words 'don't worry' to me. It was almost as if she had planned for this scenario, and she didn't seem the least bit flustered.

When the doors closed and the train accelerated out of the station, the brunette immediately took a step back and pressed her hips into my ass. My eyes flung open as I looked at her in the window. There was a hard object in her pants that felt suspiciously like a cock. I knew she wasn't transgender—I'd already felt all of her lady parts close up the previous day. Was it a vibrator, a cucumber, or some other kind of sex toy? Whatever it was, I was instantly turned on by the thought of being penetrated by her. This upped the danger quotient considerably, and my pussy was already watering in anticipation.

She unbuttoned her suit jacket and I saw her reach between her legs to make an adjustment. The girls on the bench in front of me widened their eyes, and I wondered if they could see the object between the brunette's legs. The brunette raised my dress a few inches then I felt a hard piece of rubber slap up against my vulva. I drew in a gasp of air, instantly recognizing the familiar shape. But this was no ordinary dildo, because both of the brunette's hands were otherwise occupied. Her left hand grasped the overhead bar next to mine and her right hand was resting on my hip.

What the fuck? I thought, my forehead wrinkling in confusion.

Then the brunette began to move her hips and removed all doubt.

It was a strap-on dildo! Holy shit—she planned to fuck me straight up under my dress in plain view of all the other passengers!

She tilted her hips upward trying to angle the tip of the dildo into my pussy, but she didn't have enough leverage to slip it in. She looked at me in the window and nodded, asking for an assist. I glanced at the other passengers seated on the bench in front of me and saw they were all busy tapping on their phones. I reached under the front of my dress pretending to scratch my leg and pushed the tip into my opening. The brunette took care of the rest, angling her hips and pressing forward.

The six-inch dildo quickly filled my pussy, and my eyelids flitted closed as I grunted in pleasure. The girls in front of me couldn't have seen the dildo entering me under my dress, but the action of the brunette's hips made it crystal clear exactly what was going on. The motion of her hips was unmistakable. This time she wasn't just rubbing her mound against the back of my ass, this was her full-on fucking me with a strap-on dildo!

The feeling of the hard rubber cock inside me was sublime. This was the one thing I'd missed on our previous days' trysts, and I rocked my hips gently to meet the brunette's thrusts. My lubrication was already soaking the phallus, and I could hear the faint sloshing sound it made every time the brunette rammed it into me. Some of the other passengers on the bench looked up and twisted their heads trying to detect where the sound was coming from, and the brunette slowed her pace until they looked back down at their phones.

I could feel the cock pushing and pulling my labia as it stretched the hood of my clitoris over my erect nub. The NYU girl kept looking up from her phone then back down again to type on her screen. Whether her hands were too busy texting to touch herself, or she was too engrossed in the obvious online chat she was having with her friends, was unclear. But either way, it added to the sexual tension. Although she wasn't stimulating herself like she was yesterday, I now had four voyeurs watching me instead of two.

Just as I began to feel the pleasure intensity rising in my womb, the train roared into the 96th Street station. The brunette paused again as the passengers thinned out around us and began exiting the cabin. But the feeling of having her hot poker inside me while everybody went about their everyday business was surreal, and my pussy pulsed in excitement. I was glad when a new round of passengers crowded into the compartment that nobody got up to leave the bench in front of me. I'd have the same group of distracted travelers for at least one more stop.

When the train left the station, I squeezed the brunette's hand on the overhead rail to signal I was ready for her to get me off. She nodded, then looked down at the texting girls as she slammed her rubber cock deep into my pussy. I staggered forward, almost falling on top of the passengers, and apologized for the movement of the train shifting me off balance. The three girls looked up at me and smiled slyly, knowing what had happened.

I was standing directly over them now and could see their phone screens clearly. As the brunette began to pick up her pace and slap the dildo in and out of me, I caught snippets of their online conversation.

Fuck that's hot! the NYU girl typed.

Can u believe this is happening right in front of us? one of the other girls replied.

Do u think anyone else besides us is noticing? the other one said.

Not that I can tell, the NYU girl replied, then she paused for a moment. *Are you guys getting as turned on as I am?*

Fuck, yes! her friend replied. *I want that thing inside me too!*

I'm gonna cum just watching these two, the other one said.

Knowing the girls were getting just as worked up as I was from our clandestine encounter made me even more aroused than before. I knew it wouldn't be long now before I came, and I peered at the brunette in the window to signal I was close. She removed her other hand from the overhead rail and placed it on the other side of my hips, then she pulled me toward her with her two hands and rammed the dildo even deeper into me. It had a slight downward curve, and it rubbed against my G-spot whenever she retracted it.

I could hear the echo in the distance from the approaching next station, but it didn't matter. My vagina was already tenting in preparation for a powerful orgasm, and I prepared myself for the impending climax. I spread my legs wider on the floor of the car and grasped the overhead bar with two hands. I could no longer keep my mouth closed as I panted with increasing urgency directly over the NYU girl's head, blowing her stray hairs to the side.

OMG, I'm gonna cum! she typed on her screen, as she squirmed on her seat.

That was enough for me, and I groaned as the first waves of my orgasm rolled over me. I clenched the rubber dildo and squeezed it as hard as I could as the walls of my love box spasmed in pleasure. I was glad my face was angled down over the girls' heads because it would have been impossible to mask the obvious pleasure I was experiencing to anyone else who might be watching. As my hips convulsed in uncontrolled spasms, the NYU girl's stomach tightened and she let out a tiny squeak.

At that moment, the train roared into the 86 Street station, and I felt a whoosh of fresh air rush into the cabin from a crack in the window. The sensation of the train filling the station echoed the feeling I was having from the rubber cock embedded in my pussy, and I grasped the overhead bar tightly as the NYU girl and I watched each other come, until we were thoroughly spent.

4

MÉNAGE À TROIS

As I stood over the college girls trying to catch my breath, I noticed the NYU girl's screen suddenly light up with new messages.

I can't wait to get off this train, one of the girls texted. *I need to touch myself right NOW!*

That's the hottest sex I've ever seen, the other one said.

What did I tell you guys? the NYU girl replied. *These are two hot mamas!*

When the train screeched to a halt, the brunette retracted the rubber dildo from between my legs, then calmly lifted it under her jacket and fastened the button. As the train began to take on a new round of passengers, the NYU girl typed a new message.

I'm going to try something, she said. *Will you guys squeeze together and take my seat?*

What are you planning to do? one of her friends replied.

You'll see.

Suddenly, the NYU girl stood up directly in front of me and turned around to face the bench, placing her hand on the bar next to mine. She caressed my hand with her fore-finger then looked me straight in the eyes in the window. Apparently, this college girl wasn't as shy as I thought. I glanced at the brunette in the mirror and we nodded, recognizing what she wanted. I stepped in front of her and the brunette moved behind her, sandwiching the NYU girl between us. Her two girlfriends stopped texting on their phones and looked up at the three of us, wondering what we had planned.

When the train left the station, the brunette and I pressed our bodies tightly together, then I saw her unclasp her jacket and fumble between her legs to free the rubber dildo. She lifted one side of the girl's skirt then tilted her hips upward just as she'd done with me. I saw the girl's eyes widen in the window reflection as she felt the cock suddenly flap between her legs. But in her sandwiched position, it wasn't as easy for her to reach between her thighs to help point it where it belonged.

I moved my hand around the side of my hips and reached under the front of her skirt. The girls in front of me sat ram-straight in their seats, watching in disbelief. Just as I'd hoped, the NYU girl was bare and nude under her clothes. The feeling of her wet vulva pulsing over top of the hard dildo made my own pussy throb again. I placed my fingers under the dildo and pressed it against the girl's slit, while the brunette slid it forward and back across her opening. I could feel the girl's breath on my neck as she panted from the friction of the hard phallus against her engorged clit.

The brunette and I teased the girl for a few moments, then I pressed the tip of the dildo into her pussy with my two fingers. The girl's hips tilted away from me as she pointed her hole toward the cock. When it entered her, she moaned in my ear and kissed my neck softly. I could feel the moisture returning to my own cunt and I suddenly wished I was the one getting fucked again.

I kept my hand between the girl's legs as I felt the slippery dildo sliding in and out of her. I glanced up in the window and both the brunette and I watched the girl's face twisting in pleasure. I moved my fingers to the front of her mound and located her clit and began rubbing it in circles while the brunette pushed harder against her hips. I could see the pleasure rising on the girl's face, but we only had a short interval before the next stop at 72nd Street, and we had to pause again while everybody got off the train so as not to attract too much attention.

While the brunette kept her hips locked against the girl's ass with the dildo buried inside her, I moved my hand from under the girl's skirt and placed my wet fingers on top of hers on the overhead bar. One of her friends on the bench looked up at the NYC girl and mouthed the letters 'O - M – G' to her with wide eyes. 'So hot!' she mouthed, shifting her weight uncomfortably on her seat.

The NYU girl simply gritted her teeth and looked straight ahead, not wanting to draw any extra attention to her prostrated position. I glanced at the map on the wall and saw that our next stop was Columbus Circle. We'd have a slightly longer run before our next interruption, and I nodded to the brunette in the window that this was our chance to get the girl off.

After a new crop of passengers crowded into the compartment and the train raced back into the tunnel, I reached around behind me again and grasped the rubber joystick in my hand. The size and texture of the dildo made it almost feel like a real cock, and the girl's lubrication coating the surface made it slide effortlessly in my hand. I paused for a few moments to savor the brunette's fucking action, then I returned my fingers to the girl's love button.

She had a gloriously smooth and soft pubis, and her clit was poking out of her hood like a hot chili pepper. I pinched the tip of it between my thumb and forefinger and rolled it around. The girl whimpered in my ear as she pressed her tits into my back, resting herself against me. I pushed back with my arm on the overhead rail to support us as I began to circle her clit with my fingers.

I could feel her breath coming in stronger bursts now against the back of my neck. It was exhilarating to have such a direct connection with what she was feeling. I looked in the window and saw that she was peering directly at me now, as her eyelids fluttered in waves of pleasure. The brunette sensed she was close also, and grasped the girl's hips, thrusting the dildo deeper inside. I pressed my fingers harder against her clit and began to circle it more quickly.

The girl pressed her mouth against the top of my shoulder to stifle her moans and I saw her face tighten with her impending orgasm. Suddenly, she bit into the flesh of my shoulder and I felt her hips convulse in paroxysms of pleasure. Little squeals emanated from her mouth as she panted hot breaths on my neck as her orgasm washed over her. I held my hand over her throbbing clit while her hips jerked with each orgasmic convulsion. When she finally stopped moving, the brunette and I held the girl close, savoring the three-way connection we'd just shared. I peered down at the two other girls on the bench and they simply looked up at us with their mouths agape. We'd given them a show they would never forget.

As the train roared into Columbus Circle station, I

turned around to face the girl and kissed her on her lips. The brunette withdrew the dildo from the girl's pussy and tucked it into her jacket, then she joined us in a three-way passionate kiss. We no longer cared if anyone was watching. We'd shared our own private moment of rapture, and for now at least, we were alone on our little island of ecstasy.

5

TUNNEL VISION

fter my conference ended that day, I decided to take the next two days off to explore the city. After three escalating encounters on the subway, I felt I'd exhausted all the possibilities for illicit public sex. Besides, I knew I was pushing my chances at getting caught. The widening circle of actors in our dangerous game had reached the breaking point. It was only a matter of time before someone called us out and I'd be publicly humiliated or hauled off to jail.

But I couldn't get the thought of our clandestine trysts out of my mind. Like any dangerous habit, the more you get away with it, the greater you want to stretch the limits, and the more intoxicating it becomes. I'd sampled the poison too many times, and I needed another fix. By Saturday, it was all I could think about, and I knew I had to go back on the train one last time before leaving the city.

I figured weekend traffic would be lighter than during rush-hour, but this posed both a challenge and an opportunity. On the one hand, there'd be far fewer prying eyes, and I might even be able to find a semi-private enclave on the train to take the affair to the next level. But we also wouldn't have the advantage of being tightly packed together, where we could get away with groping each other below everyone's line of sight. Plus, there was a good chance that neither the brunette nor the college girl would be using the train on the weekend.

But it didn't matter to me. I just wanted to get back on the train and relive the memory. If I found another willing partner and the opportunity presented itself, that would be a bonus. I put my sundress on one last time and strapped on some flat sandals. There'd be no need to elevate myself to gain easier access to my undercarriage if I'd no longer be standing in a crowded car. Otherwise, I was completely bare of any accessories. The idea of being naked again under my loose dress in a public place was a thrill all in itself.

After a hearty brunch at the hotel, I headed back to the 103rd Street station. When I got to the underground concourse, I was surprised how quiet it was at mid-morning. Unlike the previous days' rush hour, there were no lineups going into the turnstiles and the subway platform was almost empty. I walked to my usual spot on the platform and noticed a handsome young man tapping on his phone.

He looked up and appraised my tanned body in my sundress and smiled at me. He was wearing loose-fitting cargo shorts and a T-shirt with sandals. I could see his muscles rippling in his powerful arms as he turned toward me, and I paused to soak up his athletic figure when he returned his attention to his phone. He had long hair dangling past a small ring in his left ear to a chiseled jaw, like some kind of hipster Adonis. When he caught me checking out his tight ass, I blushed. I was glad when the train finally rolled into the station, providing a temporary distraction.

As I expected, the carriage was almost empty. A few scattered passengers sat on the open benches and one or two people stood impassively holding the vertical support bars. There was no sign of the brunette or college girl, so I took a seat on an open bench beside the door directly opposite the young man from the platform. When the train closed its doors and sped out of the station, I crossed my legs and appraised the hipster more carefully.

He had dark eyes, a long straight nose, and carved cheeks that accentuated his Abercrombie & Fitch youthful good looks. He couldn't have been much more than twenty, and as he sat on the bench tapping his phone, he reminded me of the pretty college girl from earlier in the week. His legs were slightly parted, and I stared up his thighs, trying to steal a glance under his shorts to see if I could catch any sign of his man junk.

But he seemed lost in his phone, and I began tapping my foot impatiently to gain his attention. He looked up briefly and caught me checking him out again, but this time we lingered with a long mutual stare. He ran his eyes down my body and I lifted my leg, parting my knees slightly. Now *he* was the one staring between my legs trying to steal a glance at my private parts.

I glanced around the cabin to scope the scene and noticed a middle-aged woman reading a book on the opposing bench on the other side of the door. Another twenty-something girl had her elbows swung around a support bar tapping on her phone, waiting for her next stop. Otherwise, the Adonis and I had the entire end quarter of the carriage to ourselves. But when I looked back toward him, his head was once again buried in his phone.

I raised my left leg and placed my sandal on the bench beside me, splaying my legs in an open scissor position. My dress billowed open and I rested my hand in my lap to cover my exposed pussy. The young man looked up at the movement in his periphery, then did a double take. I smiled at him, and he shifted uncomfortably on his bench. He looked at my bare legs and ran his gaze up my body, then paused at my bosom. My nipples were growing hard from his renewed attention, and I lifted my chest to press my breasts against the loose fabric of my dress.

When he looked me straight in my eyes, I knew his phone would no longer be a distraction. I glanced at his shorts and saw one side of his pant legs tenting inward. I was obviously getting him worked up, and I was enjoying my little tease. I looked at the woman across the aisle to make sure no one else was watching, then I hiked up the left side of my dress over my knee to show the young man my bare pussy.

Suddenly, the left side of his shorts began to push outwards as I saw his penis elongate along the side of his leg. He wasn't wearing any underwear either! I couldn't believe how long his organ was as it continued to creep down the side of his pant leg. By the time it stopped growing, it had to be at least ten inches in length and two inches thick. My pussy twitched involuntarily, as I imagined what it would feel like to have him buried inside me.

Like the brunette had with her pantsuit, I'd made some adjustments to my sundress, and I slipped my right hand through a narrow opening I'd cut in the side. When the young man saw my hand emerge between my legs and begin playing with my cunny, he sat up awkwardly, trying to free his painfully constricted hard-on. The head of his cock poked out the end of his pant leg, and I began to circle my clit as I licked the top of my lip teasingly.

He glanced to his side to make sure no one else was

watching, then he shimmied closer to the dividing wall beside the door and grasped the tip of his cock. He tried to rub the head awkwardly with the ends of his fingers and rocked his hips forward, trying to provide some extra friction. I spread my legs further apart to give him a better view, then moved my left hand through the slit in the other side of my dress and thrust my fingers into my open snatch.

My juices were flowing freely by now, and my hand made a nasty sucking sound as it pounded in and out of my pussy. Fortunately, the noise in the cabin from the train moving through the tunnel masked the sound for anyone further than a few feet away. The Adonis suddenly hiked up the side of his shorts and I gasped when I saw the size of his organ. Even half-unsheathed, it was longer than most other men's full-length penises.

But just as he wrapped his fist around the shaft, the train rattled into the next train station. When it stopped at the platform and new passengers began entering the compartment, he pulled his pant leg down to cover up his erection and I returned my elevated foot to the floor. An older gentleman entered the door on our end of the cabin and turned to take a seat in the far corner bench, facing me at a ninety-degree angle. The young man looked at me and frowned, knowing that our fun would be interrupted at least for a few more stops.

But my hands were still in the pockets of my dress, and I spread my legs just far enough apart for him to see my bare pussy, then I resumed touching myself. He squirmed and shuffled in his seat as he watched me finger my wet honeypot, while the old man stared straight ahead, unaware what was going on directly in front of him. I could see the young man's cock pressing against his pant leg as he rubbed it slowly under the coarse fabric of his shorts.

I felt sorry that he wasn't able to stimulate himself more directly, but he was in full view of the old man and there wasn't much he could do. I decided to have a little fun with him, and pulled my fingers out of my box then placed my hands on either side of my labia and pulled them apart. I used my pubococcyx muscles to flex the slit, teasing him to put his cock inside me. He groaned and lurched forward, trying to take some pressure off his trapped hard-on. I continued tormenting him for the next two stations, playing with myself as he looked on helplessly.

When we got to the 72nd Street stop, some more people filtered into our compartment. When two new passengers sat down on the other end of each of our benches, we both crossed our legs in frustration.

But I knew we had a longer interval before our next stop at Columbus Circle. I turned my head to look through the window into the next car and saw that it was just as busy as ours. Just then, a young teenager walked down the middle of our compartment, then opened the end door beside us and continued into the next car. I glanced at the man sitting across from me, then peered out the corner of my eyes toward the end door and back to him. He looked at me quizzically for a moment, then nodded when he understood what I was thinking.

I got up from my seat and walked to the end door and slowly lifted the latch. The sound of the noisy train barreling through the tunnel startled me, and I hesitated for a moment wondering if this was a good idea. There were no handrails to hold onto for support, only a flimsy chain flanking the gangway on both sides. I stepped through the door and turned around holding the handle for support, then closed it behind me. I was all alone now in the thundering tunnel, and the two cars pistoned back and forth as the train barreled through the dark corridor.

I looked through the glass wondering what was keeping the young man from joining me, then I saw him get out of his seat and walk toward the door. He turned the latch and stepped into the portal then closed the door behind him. We bent our knees together, trying to steady our balance over the shifting platform. I grabbed his shirt for support and looked down at the fluttering tracks racing underneath us, then I nodded to indicate we had to work quickly.

I looked through the window behind him to see if anyone was watching and was glad that everybody had redirected their attention, assuming we had passed through like the teenager. Then I turned around and placed my hands on the wall of the next car and lifted my dress over my ass. The young man got the message and unzipped his shorts then braced his feet on the narrow platform and pushed his hips forward. I felt his python slap up against the underside of my pussy, and I tilted my hips to give him freer access.

Unlike with the brunette's strap-on dildo, he didn't need a helping hand getting inside me. His springy cock quickly angled up toward my opening and I could feel the slippery head push my lips apart as he entered me. Bombarded with all the sensations from the train rocketing through the tunnel, it was the most intense feeling I'd ever felt. From the smell of the burning steel in the tunnel, to the roar of the train racing through the corridor, to the feeling of cool air rushing between my legs as the man thrust his giant cock into my pussy—I was stimulated to the maximum degree possible, in every imaginable way.

As the Adonis pounded his manhood into me, I struggled to maintain my balance on the shifting platform. I was suddenly glad we had a limited time to finish our business, and I began rocking my hips in concert with his thrusts to bring us both to completion. The young man reached through the hole in one side of my dress and lifted it higher as he cupped and pinched my breasts. If anybody was looking through the glass at the end of the compartment, they were certainly getting a hell of a show.

The Adonis began thrusting his cock with more urgency, and I could feel my own passion beginning to rise. This sex-on-a-train idea was *insane*, but I was loving every minute of it. Beyond the danger of someone reporting us, there was the distinct possibility either one of us could fall to our deaths on the tracks below at any moment.

I grasped the handle of the door in front of me and pressed my face against the glass as the man pushed and lifted me forward. I screamed in pleasure, and I saw a few people turn from inside the compartment to look in my direction. With the familiar sound of the approaching station filling the tunnel, the man pushed his other hand under my dress and grasped me hard by the side of my hips.

I could feel his cock flaring inside me and I knew he was close. With one final thrust, he pressed his pelvis hard against my ass and held me tight while I gushed all over his glorious firehose. While we glued ourselves together in spastic union, I watched the passengers standing on the adjacent platform race by the narrow opening between our two cars as the train poured into Columbus Circle station. When it finally came to a stop, the young man pulled his dripping penis out of me, zipped up his shorts, and the two of us walked nonchalantly into the next cabin, as the stunned passengers watched us exit the train.

Being caught red-handed having sex on the subway was more fun than I thought it would be.

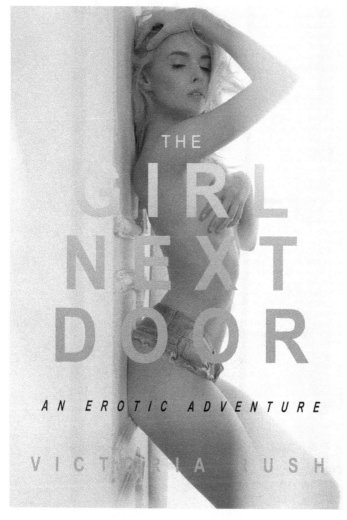

THE GIRL NEXT DOOR

AN EROTIC ADVENTURE

VICTORIA RUSH

GIRLS' CAMP

AN EROTIC ADVENTURE

V I C T O R I A   R U S H

Getting wet was never this much fun...

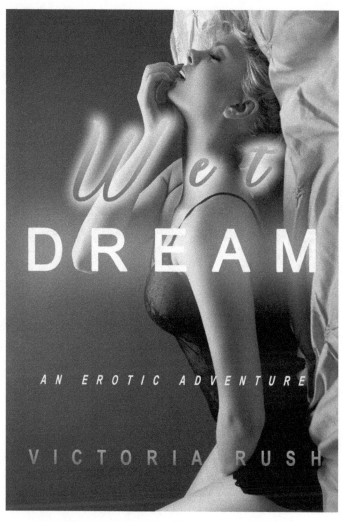

Wet

DREAM

AN EROTIC ADVENTURE

VICTORIA RUSH

There's only one place you can live out your wildest fantasies...

THE
HABIT

AN EROTIC ADVENTURE

VICTORIA RUSH

Some habits are harder to break than others...

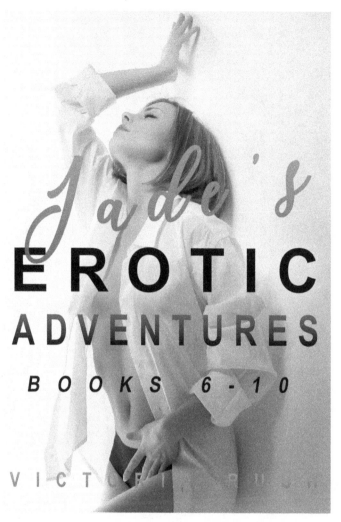

Jade's EROTIC ADVENTURES

BOOKS 6-10

VICTORIA RUSH

Books 6 - 10 in the bestselling series - now 60% off.

THE GIRL NEXT DOOR - PREVIEW
STOLEN GLANCES

In the days leading up to her parents' flight to Europe, all I could think about was Abby. She'd finally be alone, free to express herself and do anything she wanted. At the very least, I hoped she'd spend a little more time in her backyard. A late-summer heat wave had struck the city, and there'd be plenty of opportunities for her to take a refreshing dip in the pool. Maybe she'd been secretly harboring a two-piece swimsuit or — God forbid — planning a skinny-dip after dark. Either way, I'd be glued to my balcony in hopes of stealing another glance at her sweet, nubile body.

But after her parents left, I was disappointed to see her resume her sequestered ways. One day she left the house to pick up groceries and a couple of days later a middle-aged woman I presumed to be her aunt visited for a couple of hours. But during that first week, she ventured into her backyard only a few times to sunbathe in her one-piece suit. By the middle of the vacation fortnight, I began to despair of seeing any part of her beyond her bare legs.

One night as I was getting ready for bed, I noticed her

bedroom light was on later than usual. Our windows faced each other on the same side of our house, but she'd always kept her curtains drawn for privacy. Tonight though, I noticed a sliver of light emanating from a crack in the canopy. I crept up to the side of my window and separated my blinds with two fingers, then peered across the narrow laneway.

Abby was sitting at her desk, peering at a computer screen. She was wearing a light nightgown, and I could see the outline of her full breasts from the backlight of the computer through the gauzy material. The screen was flickering with some kind of moving image, but it was hard to make out what she was watching from my distance about twenty feet away. I reached into my nightstand and pulled out a pair of binoculars that I kept on hand for occasional neighbor spying.

Raising the field glasses to my eyes, I gasped when I adjusted the focus and zoomed in on her. The image on the screen was a porno, showing a man and a woman having missionary sex on a bed! I tilted my binoculars down a few inches and saw Abby had her legs spread apart with her hand moving in a strange thrusting motion between her thighs.

She's masturbating while watching the video!

I've never pulled my clothes off my body so quickly in my entire life. I stripped off my jeans and dropped my panties to the floor and immediately began circling my clit. My pussy was already soaked in excitement, as my juices ran down the inside of my legs. I struggled to steady the binoculars with my left hand as I furiously tribbed myself with my other hand.

As Abby watched the video, her mouth parted and I could see a pink flush on her cheeks. Her tits bounced up and down under her skimpy negligee as she rocked gently in her chair, while she thrust her fingers between her legs in rhythm with the lovers on the bed. I was just about to come when the man in the video lifted himself off his lover and stood by the side of the bed while she began to perform fellatio. Suddenly, Abby removed her hands from between her legs and lifted a strange green object in front of her face. It was a large cucumber!

Poor girl, I thought. *She doesn't even have a proper vibrator, having to resort to common household vegetables to get off.*

But what she did next soon made me forget about her deficiency of sex toys. She placed the end of cucumber in her mouth and began sucking on the tip, imitating what the woman was doing in the video. Then she moved her left hand back between her legs and began moving it rapidly up and down. I could see her body shaking in obvious pleasure as she sucked on the green phallus.

This girl is going to make at least one Christian college boy very happy.

The man in the video placed his hands at the side of the woman's head and began deep-throating her. I could see his butt cheeks contracting as he thrust his hips forward, while Abby mimicked his movements with her own rocking action on her chair. Suddenly the man stopped thrusting as he held the woman's head tightly against his stomach.

Abby pulled the cucumber out of her mouth and thrust it between her legs, then arched her back and moaned. I didn't realize that her window also was ajar a few inches, and the sound carried clearly over the small space between our houses. I'd hardly paid any attention to my own pleasure up to that moment, but when I saw her coming, I thrust my fingers into my snatch and gushed all over my hand, biting my lip to stifle my own screams of euphoria.

Abby rested for a minute with the cucumber still embedded in her pussy, then she grabbed the computer mouse and the screen flashed a few times before she settled on a new video. I turned my binoculars back to the monitor and noticed this time the video was of two naked women scissoring on the floor. Abby paused for a moment as I saw her eyes widen and her mouth part in surprise. Then she grabbed the cucumber with two hands and started pumping it into her cunny.

Fuck, that's hot! She likes women! Thank God.

My mind was already racing with thoughts of how I could entice her into my bed. But right now, I needed something in my *own* honeypot. I reached back down into my night table and pulled out my favorite vibrator, then I turned it on maximum and plunged it deep into my snatch. Abby and I were both fucking ourselves watching other women getting off, but suddenly Abby looked up and turned her head in my direction.

Had she noticed the movement in my window? I froze with the vibrator buzzing away in my pussy, suddenly aware that I was standing stark naked in front of my window with the shades half open. As she stared in my direction and squinted her eyebrows trying to detect any sign of intrusion, I suddenly came at the thought of her seeing me. My orgasm consumed me, and I struggled to remain motionless as my upper body quaked and quivered in powerful convulsions. I stared back at her, praying she hadn't noticed me.

When she returned her attention to her screen, I suddenly became aware of the dim glow that was being cast in my own room from my open bathroom door. I quickly walked over to the bathroom and turned off the light, then returned to the edge of the window and peered through the blinds. When I looked back up at Abby's window, she'd pulled her curtains and I could only see the faint shadow of her voluptuous body standing behind the sheers.

Fuck! I cursed.

Whether she'd been distracted by the flickering light in my room or she'd noticed me watching her, was unclear. Either way, I didn't care. I'd finally seen her magnificent body in all its glory, and we'd shared a powerful moment of pleasure together. And now that I knew she was sexually active and attracted to girls, I had other plans. I was already thinking of how I could escalate our secret rendezvous.

Read More...

ABOUT THE AUTHOR

If you would like to receive notification of new book(s) in Jade's Erotic Adventures, follow me at http://bookbub.com/ authors/victoria-rush.

If you have a moment, please post a brief review on my Amazon book page at mybook.to/sa . Even just a couple of sentences will help other readers find and enjoy this book as much as you hopefully did.

Follow, share, like, and comment at:

www.facebook.com/authorvictoriarush
www.pinterest.com/authorvictoriarush
www.twitter.com/authorvictoriarush
authorvictoriarush@outlook.com

Hope to see you again soon!